SNUGGLER'S STORY

The Homeward Journey
of an Orphaned Cat

For ages 1-101

Written by Snuggler
(translated by Joanne Austin Watts)

Illustrated by Snuggler
(with help from my lady)

CATALINA ISLAND, CALIFORNIA

With much gratitude to Jon Tusak and Jim Watson for their time and skills in helping to get this book ready for publishing.

Dedicated to my son, Ron, for his strength and faith.

In memory of my son, Cal, for his love of life and enthusiasm.

In memory of my close friend, Stephanie, for her continual inspiration.

Also dedicated to animal lovers everywhere!

PREFACE

When this little cat was orphaned, he went through many hardships. But on this journey he was spreading his love and peaceful nature. He never gave up hope of being with his family again.

Because of his gentle heart, he made a couple of odd friends that some people might think would be out of character for a cat. But he never learned to discriminate. He only knew to love everything and everyone, and to forgive the ones who weren't kind to him.

Because he was guided by love, he made an impression on everyone and in the end saved several of his friends from lonely, lost lives.

He's a humble little hero in their eyes.

And he will be in yours, too.

This is me!

Hi, my name is Snuggler and everyone says I'm a kind, gentle, beautiful boy. So I know I am. I'm going to share my story with you, okay? By the way, we cats (and lots of animals) understand most of what you say in all languages. We wonder why you don't understand US. We try really hard to talk to you and sometimes some of you seem to understand in other ways, like how we act and stare at you. We think that's funny so we do that a lot.

I'm an older boy, a little out of shape.
So not as fast as when I was younger,
and only have three teeth because my
other teeth fell out when I was
homeless. But that's okay too because
I'm still very handsome and always try
to have a big smile. I've always been a
very nice boy even though there were
some hard times and I was sad.

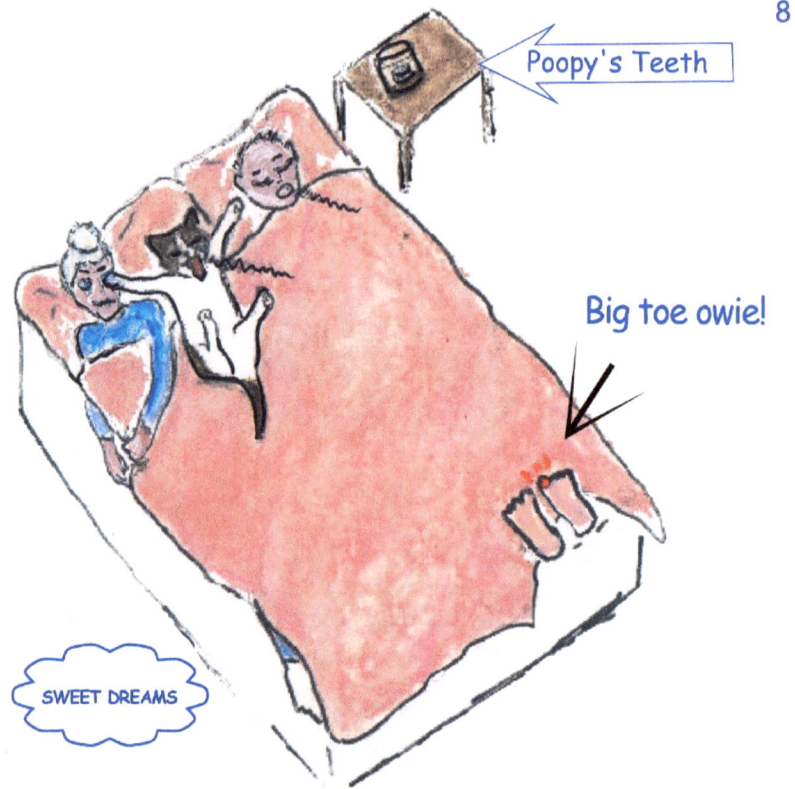

I lived with my Mummy and Poopy (that's what they called themselves) from the time I was a baby, as far back as I can remember.

They were beautiful too. They had white hair and lots of teeth and Poopy would take his teeth out at night before we went to bed and he would put them in a glass of water next to the bed so I could drink water from it if I got thirsty at night. I always slept with them and kept warm and comfortable and happy. During the day we would play and laugh a lot.

9

Why did they take Poopy?
Now Mummy is so lonely..

Mummy and me watching TV

One morning Poopy didn't get up. Then some men came and carried him away while he was sleeping. Mummy was so sad. She cried but people told her Poopy was in a place called heaven and they would be together again some day.

Pretty soon she started playing with me more and talking to me again and hugging me all the time. I would snuggle with her more and she would try to play ball with me and that would make her laugh. I never could figure that game out. I would watch her roll the ball and then she would roll it again and go get it and roll it again but she seemed to be having fun.

Then another morning those same men came and carried Mummy away too and I heard one of them say she had gone to heaven to be with Poopy. I don't know why they didn't take me too. I wanted to be in heaven with Mummy and Poopy but I didn't know where heaven was. I was so sad and lonely without them. It got dark and they didn't come home to snuggle with me in bed so I got up and decided to go find heaven.

I had never been out of our little house,
but I was hungry, too. So I knew when I
found them they would feed me and take
care of me and love me like they always did.
There was a window open, so I jumped out.
It was a long way down and I grabbed the
tree outside on the way down. I'm brave
and smart, but I didn't know what those
big things were that were going by real
fast, but I stayed away from them. I
learned later they are called cars.

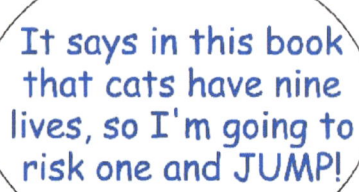

I looked everywhere and walked a long way looking for Mummy and Poopy but then it got dark again and cold. I saw a man going into a house so I thought I could go in with him to get warm, and maybe he would share his food with me. Because when Mummy and Poopy were eating their food they would tell me if I would be a patient boy and wait for them to finish eating that they would share their food, as a special treat, so I would always be a good boy and wait because I knew what share and patient meant. Well, that man had never learned that, and he shooed me away and yelled at me like he was mad, and I don't know why he was mad at me but I ran away from there real fast. He was scary.

I kept running until I came to a big water with great big rocks by it, so I hid behind one of the big rocks and fell asleep. I was real tired because I hadn't had a catnap all day. I'm used to lots of catnaps. It was light when I woke up and then I saw lots of other cats waking up and running around the rocks. I asked one of them if she knew where heaven was, but she didn't know and didn't know what a Mummy or Poopy was and didn't even know humans snuggled. She had always lived in the rocks and was afraid of humans. She was a nice cat and I was sad for her and the other cats, but I knew I had humans that snuggled and I wouldn't give up hope and I would just keep looking until I found them. I knew they were in heaven, so I just had to find out where that was.

I was hungry and thirsty. So I went to the
edge of the big water for a drink. I put
my paw in it and tasted it, but it tasted
really bad. I saw one of the cats chase
and eat a tiny little mouse. I could never
do that because it wasn't even fair. The
cat was so much bigger, but I guess that's
all those cats have to eat when they are
hungry. I wasn't that hungry- yuck!
So I searched all day and roamed around
between all the houses and slept under
them at night.

I found my way back to where I lived and where I was
happy with Mummy and Poopy. I thought maybe they
had come back because I could hear noise inside and
they would be so happy to see me safe and at home. I
scratched on the door just a little. A human lady opened
the door and said "Scat Cat!" and shooed me away. I
didn't think she was nice either. I had lived in that
house before she did, but she didn't know that. Because
she's mean like that man was, she will probably never
find heaven.

19

So I ran again and came to a big dirt place with lots of those cars sitting in it and backs of houses all around it. Every house had a big can in back of it where the humans were throwing food and stuff in those cans almost every night. I would jump in the cans and find something to eat. I don't know what I was eating, but I was always hungry and I didn't care anymore. I was getting skinny and needed to eat something, but not little mice. I guess it wasn't healthy food like Mummy and Poopy fed me because my teeth started falling out and I was tired a lot more, but during the day I would still go searching, but I came back to the lot every night and lived like that for a long time.

Then one day while I was out searching, I came to a different big lot with houses around it and an old church at one corner of the lot. I saw some cats in a little place between a house and the church and I saw a lady feeding the cats and petting them and talking nice to them. I wondered if she would be nice to me, too. I was really lonely. So I went up real slow behind the other cats. I think I was still handsome, but maybe not as beautiful as I was a long time ago because I didn't have many teeth and wasn't such a big boy, but I still had a big head and I tried to smile, but my ears went back on their own, just in case she yelled at me, so I could be ready to run.

21

I just stayed there and watched her, but I didn't try to eat any of the food. The lady watched me too, until the other cats finished eating and there was some food left. Then she smiled at me and said "you can eat this since you know how to be patient and share and smiled at me and so glad and tomorrow I'll bring extra food for you". I was so happy that she was nice to me and so glad Mummy and Poopy had taught me how to be nice and share. I never forgot that, because I'm pretty smart as you know. I waited and slept there until the next day when the other cats came back. The lady came back again and brought more food. I waited again until the other cats ate. Then I ate good food until I was all full. I slept under those houses and she came every day and fed us and talked to us and would scratch their heads but I always stayed in back and waited because I knew she would bring enough for me too, but I didn't want to make her mad at me.

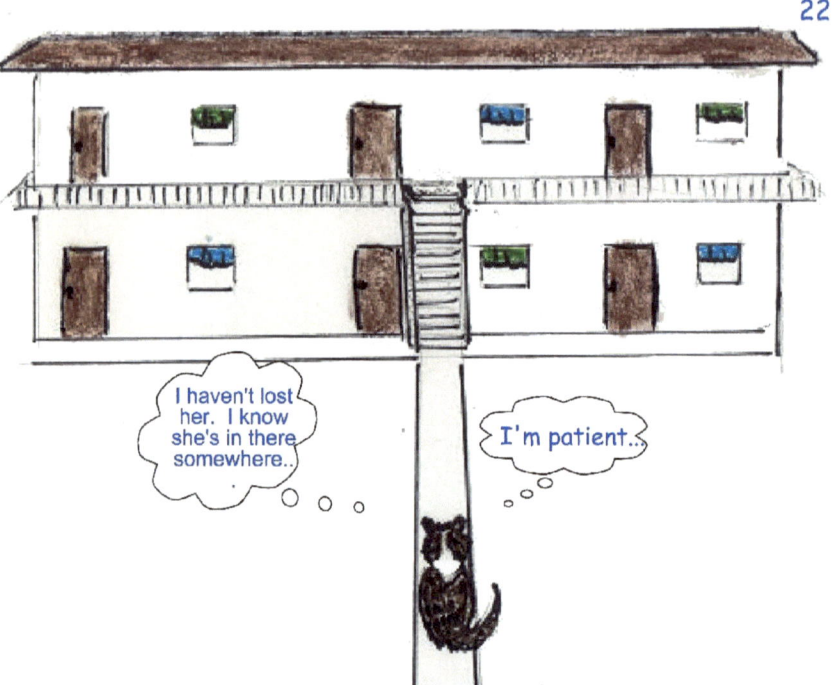

I wasn't hungry anymore. But I never forgot Mummy and Poopy and how happy we had been playing and snuggling with each other. I still had hope. The lady was real nice so I thought she might know where heaven was because that's where nice people go. So after she fed us one day, I followed her. She didn't know I was behind here. I didn't have to go very far, but I did have to stop and watch out for those big cars going fast. So I almost lost her, but I did see her go to a big house and up some stairs. But there were lots of doors and I didn't see which one she went in. Other humans were going in and out of the other doors and one of them shooed me away. So I ran down the stairs to a big room where a lot of cars were sitting still. There was an alley behind that big room so I went out there. I knew the lady was somewhere in that big house and I don't give up easy, so I went all around it.

23

Looking for her going in or out of a door, I remembered she had gone up some stairs, so I was looking up when I saw her up on a high place with a fence around it and then she went in a door up there. Now I know where she was! It got dark again so I went in that big car room and slept in a car. Then when it started to get light I went back out to the alley and waited and watched. It was too high up for me to climb and I wasn't as strong as I used to be when I was hanging from that tree. I'm a very quiet boy with a soft voice and don't talk much, but I tried to call the lady.

I had heard the other cats holler really loud sometimes so I tried to do that. Over and over I tried and suddenly a real loud scream came and it was out of *ME*. It scared me at first, but I kept doing it now that I knew how. The lady came running out and looked down and saw me.

She said, "What are you doing here? Stay there!"
She came down through the big car room where I had
slept, with some food and water, and sat down on the
ground with me to talk to me and kept petting my
head and I snuggled against her. I was so happy! She
gave me some big hugs and called me Snuggler and
that would be my name from then on and she would be
MY lady. She told me there were rules for the big
house so she couldn't let me come inside, but she
would feed me and take care of me and find me a
good home because I was a smart, nice beautiful boy.
She put a soft blanket in the car room way in the
back, and fed me and talked to me and snuggled with
me every day.

I was so happy to have a nice lady to be with again and someone to like me and pet me and help me to find a happy home, again.

Pretty soon she did find me a home with a nice man not far from where she lived. He would feed me and let me stay inside when it was dark and cold and I liked him, but I did miss my lady and Mummy and Poopy. Then one day I wanted to go inside my new house where the man was, but he wouldn't open the door. Pretty soon my lady came and carried me back to her big house. She told me that the man had gone to heaven. I guess all nice people and animals go to heaven and I try to be real nice so some day I'll get to go there, too.

My lady told me "I wish I could let you come inside with me so we could be together all the time, but the rules won't let me. But I'm going to take good care of you outside anyway, so don't you worry." She would put fresh water and a bowl of warm food outside her door every morning and night and during the day she would put me up on an old table by her door and snuggle and talk to me. We would look in each other's eyes and I knew she loved me and I told her I loved her with my eyes and I knew she understood. She had told me I was such a good, kind boy and said she could understand what I was thinking through my eyes and I was always quiet because I knew humans don't understand what we say like we understand them.

27

I followed my lady everywhere unless she said "No, Snuggler, you stay." Unless she said that to me, I was right behind her when she went to the laundry room, took out her trash , or anywhere else around the big house. People around here would laugh at me, but I didn't care. But when she went across the street she would say to me real loud, "No Snuggler, you stay!", so I knew what "No" and "stay" meant, and I never wanted her to be mad at me. Sometimes I would wait and it seemed like she would be gone a long time and I would worry that she had gone to heaven and I wanted to know where it was just in case she didn't come back, so I would know how to find her and of course Mummy and Poopy. I loved my lady but I hadn't forgotten about them. I think my lady knew that because she told me ont time, " You must have had a very kind, loving family for you to be such a good, special boy". She said "I'm sure they would have taken you with them if they would have been able to and never forget them and to remember they loved me."

I was very curious to know where she was going anyway, so I did follow her one day. I was careful and watched and waited for all the fast cars to go first. I didn't have to go very far because I found her by that church feeding the cats I used to eat with. I was so happy she was still feeding my friends because they had shared with me.

29

I was so happy that I rubbed against her legs, but she looked down and when she saw me she scolded me. She picked me up though and carried me home, so I knew she wasn't real mad. She just wanted to keep me safe. And I was a big heavy boy again and it was so much fun having my lady carry me home. I was sure she loved me because she wasn't that mad. The next day I thought "That was so much fun, I'll follow her again." Like always, she said "Stay, Snuggler", but when she got where I couldn't see her, I hurried after her, but she was hiding and waiting to see if I was going to follow her again.

She's pretty smart too! she chased me hollering "Nooo!" at me and she acted really mad at me so I ran back to the house. I won't do it again because I want her to love me and be happy with me, not mad at me, and I'm smart and she knows that I know what "stay" and "nooo" mean.

31

Now I wait with patience for her in front of the big house even if I have to wait all day. Then when she comes back she always says "What a good boy you are, Snuggler." and that makes me feel really good. The other humans would see me waiting and laugh more and say I acted like a dog. Whatever they mean by that, I don't know. They acted like it was a good thing though. Dogs are smart, but cats are just as smart.

Then one day the boss of the building came and told my
lady she couldn't keep me because it was against the
rules. My lady told her the man had gone to heaven and
I was getting older and I didn't have anyone to feed me
and take care of me, so the boss said I could stay until
my lady found me a home, but I couldn't go inside. A
few days later, the boss came back with a girl. They all
sat at our old table talking about me. The girl was real
nice to me and hugged me and she talked to me. I knew
she liked me and told my lady she wanted to take me
home with her, but she lived far away across the big
water and in the mountains. My lady said she was afraid
I would wander away and get lost or hurt, but the girl
said she would keep me inside and take good care of me.
My lady talked to the girl a long time and asked her a lot
of questions. The boss was sitting right there and the
girl was saying nice, good things. My lady didn't know
what to say.

33

She had tears going down her face because she loved me and didn't want me to go, but she ran out of questions and the girl was nice and the boss was there so she told the girl she could take me. She hugged me, and walked inside her door.

Then the boss and the girl put me in a box with holes in it. They were going to take me far away. I wanted to stay with my lady even if I had to stay outside forever. I was in the box and the box was still on the table in front of my lady's door. So I tried to get out, but it was locked and I couldn't.

But then I remembered something and
what it meant, and with all my might I
started hollering "Nooo!, Nooo!, Nooo!,
Nooo!", over and over as loud as I could
and they really understood what I was
saying and that I knew what I was saying.
They believed me and they let me out of
the box and knocked on my lady's door.
When she came out she had more tears on
her face and when she saw me standing
there out of the box, she picked me up
and hugged me.

They told her what happened and that I really meant "No, I didn't want to go", and that I wanted to stay with my lady. They said they were really surprised at how smart I am. Now I know that being smart is important. I never really knew why, but it got me out of the box and back with my lady. Then the girl was sad and had tears on her face, so my lady gave her a hug and said she was sorry and thanked her and the house boss.

The boss just said "It was meant to be, but you must remember to bring his bowls and bed inside when the bigger bosses come and we'll hope nobody complains." Bigger bosses? Uh oh!

37

Then a new cat came and started eating out of
my bowls. She was real pretty and nice. She
was older and only had one eye and not many
teeth either. She said someone mean had
chased her with a stick and it poked her eye
out and it really hurt for a while, but it didn't
hurt anymore. That mean person won't go to
heaven. She told me she had a nice man like
Poopy who she used to live with, but he had
gone to heaven and now she was homeless and
always hungry. I told her not to worry, that I
would share my food with her and some day
we would find heaven where only nice people
live. But when my lady saw her she said she
couldn't stay here because the boss would see
her and we would all get in trouble and have to
move or I would have to go away. But then my
lady could see the girl cat was hungry and
didn't have anybody taking care of her, so she
started feeding her soft warm food at a
vacant lot next door. It had an old wood box
on it and she put blankets in it for her and a
lid. She named her Wani for one eye.

This is where Wani
lives and where my
lady feeds her

TAILS OF THE HEART

Wani and I were good friends and we would play and chase each other around the big house when all the humans were asleep at night. We would eat, catnap, and play, but my lady thought I was lonely. She didn't know we were playing together and pretty happy.

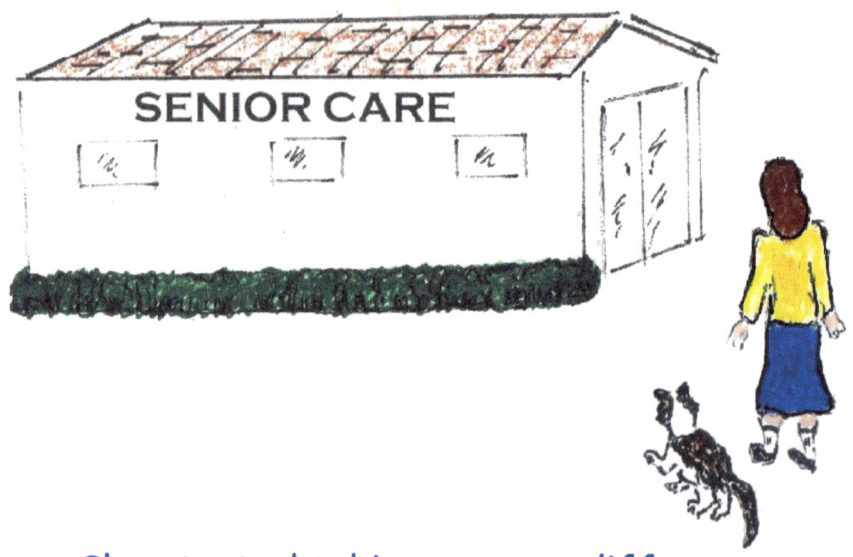

She started taking me to a different building with people in beds in all different rooms. They had white hair and I think they were lonely. I would snuggle with them and they would smile and look happier and that made me feel real good, too. Then they started leaving. Not all at once, but one at a time, and I heard someone say "They went to heaven, too." When I find heaven, I'll see all those nice people, again...

and Mummy and Poopy....

My lady quit taking me there because it started being cold all the time and water would come down hard from the sky and the trees would be blowing around. My lady was so worried about me and would put warm blankets over my box. She was so sorry when the big bosses came and she had to take my box inside.

I know how sad that made her,
but I was OK. I would snuggle
against the door so I wouldn't
blow away and Wani would stay
in her box. I had never been so
cold, though, and had never seen
so much water come down from
the sky, but I made it OK and it
started to get warmer, again.

43   It finally got warmer and I was fine and my lady and I would sit at the table again. This time it was different than it used to be. She was always writing something while she was talking to me. It must be a human game.

On warm, sunny days, my lady would sit me on the table and talk to me, again. She told me "Snuggler, you won't have to go through another winter outside like that ever again. We are going to do something about it." So every nice day, she would put me on the table and talk to me and look real long in my eyes. But I could look longer because she would blink and I don't. Then she would write something on paper. It was like a game, and we did that over and over, day after day, for a long time. She had told me "I know you have a story in you, Snuggler, and we're going to tell it." I didn't know what she meant, but she did, and we were having fun because we were playing the game together.

I guess she got tired or writing so we didn't do that part of the game any more, but she would still come out and talk to me and snuggle. I was real happy and it was nice and warm again and Wani was okay too because she had lived in her warm box with warm food when it was so cold. Now we played and chased each other like we did before and everything was good again.

45

Then one day some men came and went in my
lady's door and started carrying out tables,
chairs, and boxes, and my lady's bed. I was so
afraid they were going to take my lady out and
take her to heaven. I ran down to the big room
where the cars were parked. I thought I would
wait and if they put my lady in the big car I
would chase after them. I was so sad and afraid
because I didn't want to be alone without her. I
stayed there until it got dark and the men all
left in the big car with all my lady's things but I
didn't see them take my lady.

I didn't know what to do or where to go. I
went back upstairs but the door was closed
so I ran back down to the big room to watch
for the men again. I guess I was crying
because water was running off my face. They
must have taken her to heaven first while I
was playing and now I don't know how to find
her either. I had never been so sad. I just
curled up in the corner and cried and cried.

47

What's that? It sounds like my lady's voice...

I'm sorry, Snuggler.

But then I thought I heard my name. I got up and listened and I heard my lady's voice- I did!, I did! I heard her calling, "Snuggler, Snuggler, where are you?"? I ran up the stairs. She picked me up and held me and hugged me tight. She put me on the table and I was running around in circles and I almost fell off.

I had never, ever, been so happy. She said,
I'm so sorry Snuggler, but I was so busy
packing that I forgot you might be scared and
I forgot to tell you what we're doing. But
don't you worry, good boy, because we are
moving to a house where you and Wani can
come inside and not be cold any more.
Remember I told you that you wouldn't have
to be outside another winter? You helped me
write your story and people bought your story
and gave us enough money to buy our own
house where we can all live together."

We have our own door now and we have one of those cans in back of our new house, but no cats have to eat out of it.

We didn't move very far away from the big house, but it's ours and we have our own door so we can go in and out whenever we want. That's me, Wani, and our friends from the lot. My lady brought them home to live with us. So we can keep warm and play together and we can all sleep together with my lady.

I'm so happy now with my lady and all my friends because I love her and all of them.

My lady says we should always say our prayers and be thankful for every day that we are together.

We all sleep together and are comfortable and warm and we all purr from happiness. I think my Lady is really happy too because she purrs even louder than Mummy did.

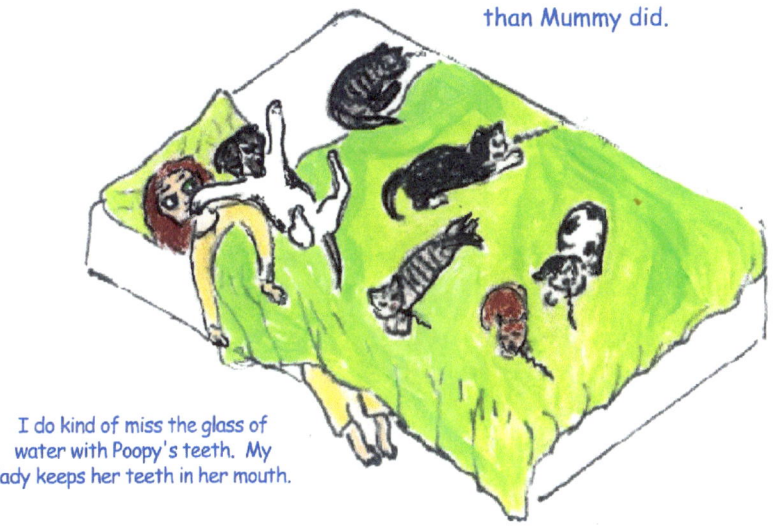

I do kind of miss the glass of water with Poopy's teeth. My lady keeps her teeth in her mouth.

I'll find Mummy and Poopy in heaven someday and all the nice people because that's where all loving, kind people go to be together. I'm so happy now with my lady and friends because I love her and all of them.
So remember to be kind, share , and always have hope.
Don't ever give up hope. Don't ever give up. I didn't.

Love, from Snuggler

p.s.: My lady found us a nice godmother just in case she goes to heaven before we do.
p.s.s.: Oh! I forgave those people that were mean to me, too. They may have been having a bad flea day. I know how that used to upset me.

So, Forgive!

ABOUT THE AUTHOR

Joanne Austin Watts was born in Los Angeles, California, and raised on Catalina Island off the coast of Southern California. She has operated a number of businesses in Southern California, including a successful restaurant on Catalina. In her spare time she has performed volunteer work for various charities. Despite her busy lifestyle, she managed to raise two sons (along with numerous animals).

www.ingramcontent.com/pod-product-compliance
Lightning Source LLC
Chambersburg PA
CBHW041029170626
46815CB00001B/23